The Stubborn Prince

Written by Ciaran Murtagh

Illustrated by William Álvarez

Collins

Chapter 1

There once was a prince named Magnus who was a bit
of a know-it-all. He liked to do things his own way.
Even if sometimes people knew how to do things better,
Magnus wouldn't listen.

His dad, the king, was always trying to give him advice. He'd tell him the best way to make a bed, the best way to tie his boots and the best way to brush his teeth.

The king wasn't trying to be bossy – he was just trying to pass on the things he'd learnt to his son. Magnus didn't see it that way.

Magnus was fed up with being "bossed around". As far as he was concerned, nobody told him what to do. What was the point of being a prince if you couldn't do what you wanted? He decided it was time to pack up his things, leave the castle and make his own way in life. As his dad waved him away, he gave Magnus one last piece of advice: "Don't work for any giants!"

Magnus couldn't believe his ears. "There you go again!" he said. "Telling me what to do! The sooner I'm out of here, the better!" Magnus marched out of the castle and set off to find his fortune.

He decided he wanted to get far away from his father and his kingdom, so Magnus set sail for the land across the sea.

When Magnus's ship neared land, he saw a huge castle in the distance. "That's the place for me!" he thought to himself and headed towards it.

As he walked, he passed a farmer, working in a field. "Who owns that castle?" asked Magnus.

"Oh!" replied the farmer. "Don't go there – it belongs to a fearsome giant."

Magnus laughed; he wasn't afraid of giants and he wasn't going to be told what to do. He marched straight up to the giant's door and gave it a big loud knock!

Chapter 2

Giants don't get many visitors. They're smelly, untrustworthy and always very grumpy. Why would anyone want to visit them, let alone work for them?

Magnus didn't care. He thought he knew better. Everyone else might be silly enough to be scared of giants, but he most definitely wasn't. Anyway, everyone knew that giants had piles of gold hidden away. He gave the door another loud knock.

"All right! All right!" growled a voice. "I'm coming!"

The giant opened the door and glared at Magnus. "What do you want?" he snarled.

Magnus smiled at the giant. "I'd like a job, please," he said, politely.

The giant looked Magnus up and down. "Hmmm.
I could do with a new worker. All the others ran away
or got eaten or something – " he muttered.

"What!?" said Magnus.

"Nothing," said the giant.

The giant gave Magnus a trial job for the day. He had to clean out the dung in the stable. If he did it before the end of the day, he could have a job and a place to stay. Magnus laughed. He may have been a prince, but he'd been cleaning dung out all his life. Or, at least, he'd seen other people doing it. Magnus was sure he knew the very best way.

Before he went off to tend his goats, the giant gave Magnus one last instruction. "Don't go snooping about my castle or else you'll be for it."

No sooner had he gone than Magnus began to think. Cleaning out dung would take no time at all. And, more importantly, the giant had told him *not* to do something. Nobody told Magnus what he could and couldn't do. Before he went to the stable, he decided to snoop about the castle. Magnus found all sorts of strange and wonderful rooms, but in the kitchen he found a strange and wonderful person.

Kara was the giant's maid. She was pleased to have some company, and they talked and talked until Magnus noticed the time.

"I'd better go to the stable and clean out the dung," he said.

On hearing this, the maid nodded, and then gave Magnus a piece of advice. "Shovel with the handle. It sounds strange, but if you shovel any other way, ten forkfuls of dung will replace the one you just shovelled out."

Magnus had never heard anything so ridiculous! Kara was clearly having a joke with him. Besides, he knew how to do things, and hadn't he just left home because his dad kept giving him advice? Magnus would show her.

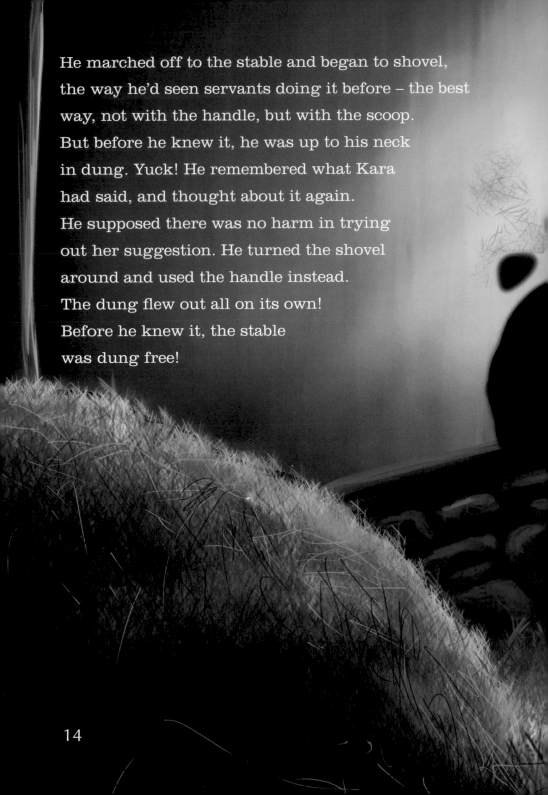

He marched off to the stable and began to shovel,
the way he'd seen servants doing it before – the best
way, not with the handle, but with the scoop.
But before he knew it, he was up to his neck
in dung. Yuck! He remembered what Kara
had said, and thought about it again.
He supposed there was no harm in trying
out her suggestion. He turned the shovel
around and used the handle instead.
The dung flew out all on its own!
Before he knew it, the stable
was dung free!

When the giant returned, he was suspicious. He asked who'd told Magnus to shovel the dung like that. He hadn't been snooping around the castle, had he?

Magnus shook his head. "No, there was no snooping from me," he replied. "Now, if you don't mind, I'm awfully tired!" And with that, Magnus went to bed.

Chapter 3

The next day, Magnus woke early and the giant
gave him another job to do before he went out into
the fields to tend his goats. He was to fetch the giant's
favourite horse from the paddock and leave it outside.
Magnus could hardly believe his ears – was that all!?
All this time he'd been bossed around by the king
– do this, do that – and here was this giant who
EVERYBODY said couldn't be trusted, giving him
the easiest life ever! He couldn't help but smile.

Before he went, the giant warned Magnus one more time not to go snooping around the castle. Magnus promised not to snoop, but no sooner had the giant closed the front door than he ran straight to the kitchen to talk to Kara.

Once again, they chatted all morning, until Magnus remembered the job he had to do. He told Kara all about the horse he had to fetch. Kara went pale.

"That horse is a ferocious beast," she said. "The only way to fetch it down is to hold the reins out in front of you, like this – "

Kara took the reins and showed Magnus what to do. Magnus laughed. He'd never heard anything so ridiculous. He'd put reins on horses before – or at least, he'd seen his servants do it – and that was definitely not the way it was done. He'd show Kara how to do it properly.

Magnus raced up to the paddock and there was the giant's horse. It looked as timid as a pet pony. Magnus scoffed – ferocious? Kara clearly didn't know what she was talking about! He strolled over, the reins looped over his arm, and stretched out a hand to pat the horse's neck.

No sooner had he stretched out his hand than the beast's eyes glowed red, fire flew from its nostrils and it snarled like a dragon! Magnus turned and ran, but the horse was hot on his heels! In desperation, Magnus dived into a water trough to escape.

When the horse had calmed down, Magnus remembered what Kara had said. Maybe she did know a thing or two about horses, after all. He held out the reins as she'd shown him and, as Magnus approached, the horse remained as calm and as timid as it'd been before. Magnus led it down to the castle where the giant waited.

"Any problems?" sniffed the giant.

Magnus smiled. "No problems."

The giant raised an eyebrow. "You haven't been snooping around my castle, have you?" he asked. "Or been talking to my maid, Kara?"

Magnus shook his head. "I don't know what you're talking about," he said. "Who's Kara?" And, with a smile, he headed off to bed.

Chapter 4

The next morning, Magnus woke up feeling happier than ever. Working for the giant was much better than being bossed about by his dad. He couldn't wait to hear what easy job the giant had for him that day.

When he went downstairs, the giant was waiting for him. "It's time for me to pay my taxes," growled the giant. "I want you to go to the goblin mines and collect my gold."

Magnus smiled; taking gold from goblins was as easy as, well, taking gold from goblins … He'd have that job done in no time.

Before he left, however, the giant warned him for a third time. "No snooping," he said, "or there'll be trouble."

Magnus made a solemn promise and waved the giant off. No sooner had the giant gone than Magnus laughed.

"What a fool!" he chuckled. He ran straight to Kara and sat down in the kitchen for breakfast.

As they talked, Magnus told Kara all about the job he had to do that day, and Kara gave him some advice. "When you meet the goblins," she said, "they'll ask how much gold you want. Only ask for two sacks, one for each hand."

Magnus laughed – what a silly thing to ask! He'd collect all of it! Once again, he decided not to listen to Kara and do things his own way.

Magnus marched straight down to the goblin mine and knocked on the door.

The chief goblin stuck out a furry face.
"Yes?" he snapped. "What is it?"

"I'm here for the giant's gold," said Magnus.

The goblin raised an eyebrow. "How much do you want?" he asked.

Magnus grinned. "All of it!"
he said, smugly.

"All of it?" said the goblin.
"As you wish!"

All of a sudden, nugget upon nugget of gold was flying
out of the tunnel and landing on Magnus. He was
soon neck-deep in the heavy gold chunks. He couldn't
move, and pretty soon he wouldn't be able to
breathe or speak. He remembered what Kara
had said and shouted in panic, "I mean,
just two sacks! Just two sacks! One for
each hand!"

The goblin smiled and clicked his
fingers, and suddenly Magnus
was holding two sacks of gold.
Magnus breathed a sigh of relief,
waved goodbye to the goblin and
headed back to the giant's castle.

The giant wasn't there when he returned so
Magnus went to show Kara the gold he'd carried
from the mine. But little did Magnus know that, as
they talked, the giant was spying on him through
the kitchen window.

"The little liar," snarled the giant. "I'll show him ..."

Chapter 5

The next morning, Magnus went down to meet
the giant and see what task he had for him that day.
The giant was waiting for him.

"No task today," said the giant, taking Magnus by
the hand and leading him into the kitchen where
Kara was waiting. "I believe you've already met,"
said the giant.

"Oh yes," said Magnus, before realising his mistake.
Of course, he wasn't supposed to have met Kara
at all.

"Just as I thought!" said the giant, pushing
Magnus towards Kara. "Chop him up and throw
him in my soup!" he shouted. "And wake me when
he's cooked!"

The giant went over to a long bench by the fire and
settled down to sleep. Soon, the kitchen vibrated
with the sound of his snoring. Kara took a large
cooking pot and filled it with water.

"You're not going to do it, are you?"
stammered Magnus.

Kara put her finger to her lips and pointed at the giant. "Do exactly as I tell you, and you'll be fine," she said.

Magnus was about to argue that nobody told him what to do, when he remembered all the scrapes Kara had got him out of. Perhaps she was somebody he really should be listening to, after all …

Kara popped the pot on the stove. Then she pricked her finger with a knife, and sprinkled three drops of her own blood into the pot. Magnus watched: what was she doing? That wasn't how you made soup! But for the first time in his life, he didn't say a word. Then she put some old shoe soles, a dead rat and a load of rubbish from the bin into the pot, as well. Giants just loved dead rats!

Finally, Kara took a lump of salt and a flask of water. "Come," she said. "If you want to live, we must run!" For once, Magnus didn't need telling twice. Quickly, he and Kara ran from the kitchen, hopped on to a horse and raced away.

The giant heard the noise. "Is he done yet?" he asked, sleepily.

From the pot, the first drop of Kara's blood began to speak. "Only just begun," it said.

The giant went back to sleep, and Magnus and Kara raced further away.

A little time later, the giant stirred again. "Is he ready yet?" he asked.

"Half done," answered the second drop of blood from the pot.

The giant went back to sleep, and Magnus and Kara raced even further away.

Finally, the giant stirred for the third time. "Is he ready yet?" he asked.

"Perfect! Come and get him!" said the third drop from the pot.

The giant stumbled sleepily to the pot, grabbed a ladle and tasted his soup. "Yeurgh!" he yelled, spitting out the soup. "She's tricked me! There's no boy in this pot. Where is she?"

Chapter 6

The giant jumped on his horse and gave chase.
From the horizon, Magnus looked back and saw
the flames shooting from the horse's nostrils and the giant
riding on its back. "We'll never outrun him," he said.

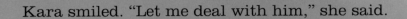

Kara smiled. "Let me deal with him," she said.

Magnus was about to argue, but then he
thought again. Kara was clearly very clever.
Perhaps it was time to trust her!

They reached the sea and Kara hopped into
a sailing boat. Soon the giant reached the shore too,
but there was no boat for him.

"I know how to handle this," he said, and he called up his cousin the Sea Slurper. The Sea Slurper took out a big straw and sucked up the sea. The boat Magnus and Kara were in was soon bouncing on the dry seabed and going nowhere. Magnus panicked.

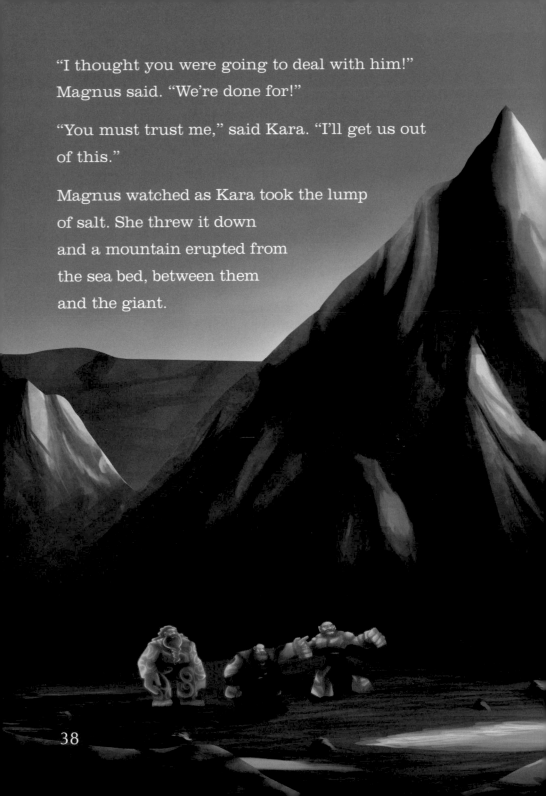

"I thought you were going to deal with him!"
Magnus said. "We're done for!"

"You must trust me," said Kara. "I'll get us out
of this."

Magnus watched as Kara took the lump
of salt. She threw it down
and a mountain erupted from
the sea bed, between them
and the giant.

"I know how to handle this," said the giant, and he called up his other cousin, the Rock Wrecker, to munch a tunnel through the rock.

Magnus and Kara ran on to the other shore, but the giant was through the tunnel and back on their heels. His cousins, the Sea Slurper and the Rock Wrecker, were right there at his side.

"This is worse than ever!" wailed Magnus.

From the safety of the shore, Kara opened the small
flask she'd taken from the kitchen and tipped out
the water. It seemed as if gallons of water were flowing
from the tiny bottle. Soon the sea was raging again.

The water swirled around the giant's legs and then
the giant's middle, until, with a mighty swoosh, a wave
knocked the giant clean off his feet. He tried to swim to
the shore, but it was no use. He was swept away with
his two cousins, never to be heard from again.

"Where shall we go?" asked Kara. "Now that we've left the giant, we've no home to go to."

"I have an idea," said Magnus.

Magnus took Kara back to his father, the king, and apologised for being such a know-it-all. If Kara had taught him anything, it was when to listen to people who knew better. His life had been saved time and time again, thanks to her. If he'd done things his own way, he'd have ended up as a giant's dinner.

His father was pleased to hear that his son had finally
learnt his lesson, and welcomed them both into
his home. Soon they were married. Kara was a good
wife and a wise princess, and Magnus a loyal husband.
And when Kara told Magnus the best way to make
the bed, tie his boots or brush his teeth, Magnus
always listened.

Clever Kara